To my grandchildren — EA

To all who are surprised by and learn from
their environment every day — MM

Groundwood Books / House of Anansi Press
110 Spadina Avenue, Suite 801, Toronto, Ontario M5V 2K4
or c/o Publishers Group West
1700 Fourth Street, Berkeley, CA 94710

We acknowledge for their financial support of our publishing program
the Canada Council for the Arts, the Government of Canada through
the Canada Book Fund (CBF) and the Ontario Arts Council.

 Canada Council
for the Arts Conseil des Arts
du Canada  ONTARIO ARTS COUNCIL
CONSEIL DES ARTS DE L'ONTARIO

Library and Archives Canada Cataloguing in Publication
Amado, Elisa, author
Why are you doing that? / by Elisa Amado ; illustrated
by Manuel Monroy.
ISBN 978-1-55498-453-4 (bound)
I. Monroy, Manuel, illustrator  II. Title.
PS8551.M335W49 2014      jC813'.6      C2013-905607-6

The illustrations were done digitally,
starting with drawings in color pencil, and watercolor.
Design by Michael Solomon
Printed and bound in Malaysia

MIX
Paper from
responsible sources
FSC
www.fsc.org   FSC® C012700

# Why Are You Doing That?

## Elisa Amado

*pictures by*

## Manuel Monroy

GROUNDWOOD BOOKS

HOUSE OF ANANSI PRESS

TORONTO  BERKELEY

"Why are you doing that?" asked Chepito as his mother stood at the stove, cooking eggs and frying beans.

"I'm making your breakfast," answered his mother.

"What for? What for?" sang Chepito.

"These eggs and beans will make you really strong."

Chepito ate as fast as he could and ran out the door.

There was his neighbor, Manuel, digging in the ground.

"Why are you doing that?" asked Chepito.

"I'm digging out the weeds that are growing around the corn," said Manuel.

"What for? What for?" sang Chepito.

"Because weeds keep the corn from growing tall and strong. Look at this nice elote," Manuel said as he peeled back the husk.

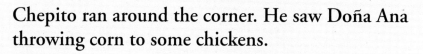

Chepito ran around the corner. He saw Doña Ana throwing corn to some chickens.

"Why are you doing that?" he asked.

"Because the chickens need to eat," answered Doña Ana.

"What for? What for?" sang Chepito.

"So that they can grow strong and lay good eggs like the ones you just had for breakfast."

Down along the road, Chepito found Juan and Dolores. They were tying plants to some sticks.

"Why are you doing that?" asked Chepito.

"To keep these plants from falling on the ground where the bugs and slugs can eat them," said Dolores.

"What for? What for?" sang Chepito.

"So that these beans can grow on the plants. See the frijoles inside? You soak them and cook them and then you eat them. Didn't you just have some for breakfast?"

Just then a cow came running down the road, pulling Ramón behind on a rope.

"Why are you doing that?" asked Chepito.

"Because I need to bring the cow home to be milked."

"What for? What for?" sang Chepito.

"Come with me and you will see," said Ramón.

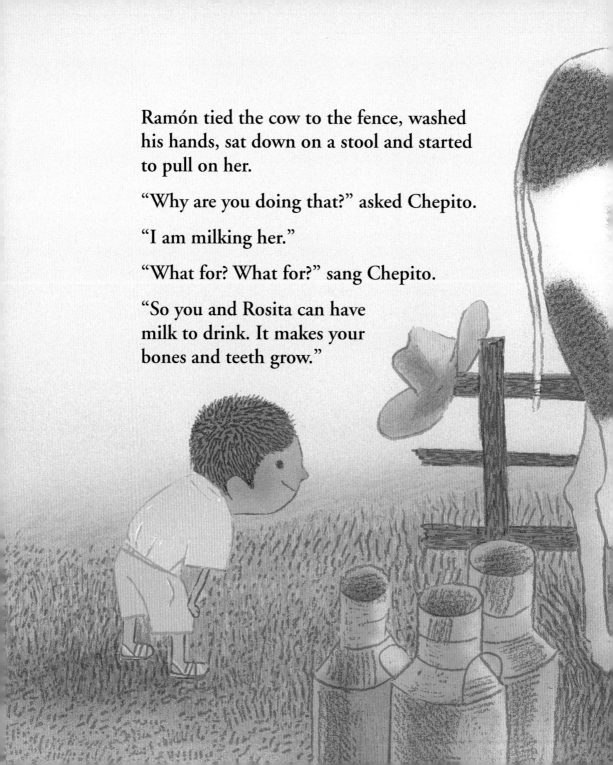

Ramón tied the cow to the fence, washed his hands, sat down on a stool and started to pull on her.

"Why are you doing that?" asked Chepito.

"I am milking her."

"What for? What for?" sang Chepito.

"So you and Rosita can have milk to drink. It makes your bones and teeth grow."

Next to the house, Maria was slapping and flattening balls of dough between her hands.

"Why are you doing that?" asked Chepito.

"Watch. I'm making tortillas," she said as she put them, one by one, on a hot comal on the fire. I made them from the corn that Manuel grows."

"What for? What for?" sang Chepito.

"You know, Chepito. So you can have them for your lunch. You'd better go home. Your mother came by and got some just a little while ago."

Chepito skipped down the road. He was hungry. He saw a bunch of bananas hanging from a tree.

"Help yourself," said a man who was lying under the tree.

"What for? What for?" sang Chepito.

"Because I can tell that you are hungry," said the man.

"Can I take one for my sister?" asked Chepito.

Chepito walked in the door. His mother and father and Rosita were already at the table.

"Come in and have some lunch," said his father.

"Are we having tortillas?" asked Chepito.

"Don't we always?" said his mother. "And some nice avocado, and chicken soup with rice."

Chepito leaned over to his sister.

"Would you like a banana for dessert?" he asked.

"Yes," said Rosita. "I love bananas. Do you?"

"Of course," said Chepito. "And you know what? They grow on a tree."

comal — a smooth, flat clay griddle used to cook tortillas
Doña — a Spanish title used before a woman's first name
elote — corn cob
frijol — black bean
tortilla — thin, round, flat bread made from cornmeal,
    cooked on a hot surface